Discarding.

Lulu's Busy Day

To Auntie Esther
with love

First published in the United States of America in 2000 by Walker Publishing Company, Inc.
First Published in Great Britain in 2000 by Orchard Books, London

Library of Congress Cataloging-in-Publication Data
Uff, Caroline.
Lulu's busy day/Caroline Uff.
p.   cm.
Summary: Lulu enjoys many activities during the day, including drawing a picture,
visiting the park, and reading a bedtime story.
ISBN 0-8027-8716-9
[1. Day Fiction.] I. Title.
PZ7.U285Lu 2000
[E]—dc21   99-36100
                                                CIP
Printed in Singapore
2 4 6 8 10 9 7 5 3 1

Lulu's Busy Day

Caroline Uff

Walker & Company
New York

Hello, Lulu.

What are you doing today?

Lulu is busy drawing.
What a beautiful picture.

Lulu likes playing ball.
Catch,
Lulu!

Lulu is off to the park.
She wears her new
colorful hat.

Look what Lulu finds...

Lulu is pretending to be a duck.

Pit pat quack quack.

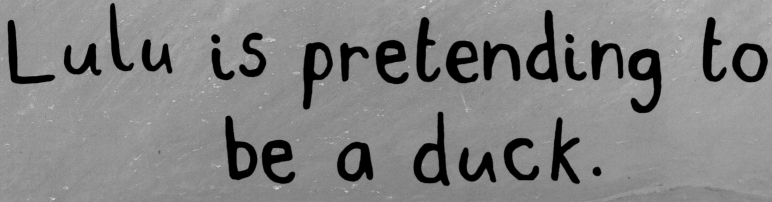

High high, high up in the sky.

Lulu plays on the swings with her best friend.

It's raining.

Splish

splash

splosh!

Time to go home, Lulu.

Lulu loves dinnertime. Yum yum.

Lulu builds houses and big castles with blocks.

Time to clean up now, Lulu.

Lulu likes lots and lots of bubbles in her bath.

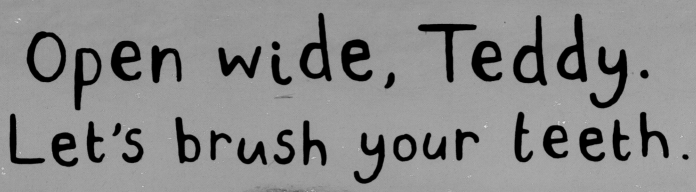

Open wide, Teddy.
Let's brush your teeth.

Lulu curls up
for a bedtime story.

Shhh!
Lulu is fast asleep.

Night-night, Lulu.